For Ronnie — *J.M.G.*

For Matthew, Ben, James, Thomas,
and for John for staying up late — *A.H.*

Text copyright © 1993 by Jeanne M. Gravois
Illustrations copyright © 1993 by Alison Hill
First published in Great Britain
by ABC, All Books for Children,
a division of The All Children's Company, Ltd.

Tambourine Books, a division of William Morrow & Company, Inc.,
1350 Avenue of the Americas, New York, New York 10019.
Printed in Hong Kong

Cataloging in Publication Data was not available in time for
publication of this book, but can be obtained from the
Library of Congress. L.C. 93-1990
ISBN 0-688-13047-X (trade)   ISBN 0-688-13048-8 (lib.)
First U.S. edition, 1994
1 3 5 7 9 10 8 6 4 2

Quickly, Quigley

JEANNE M. GRAVOIS • PICTURES BY ALISON HILL

TAMBOURINE BOOKS NEW YORK

Quigley was small.
And Quigley was slow.
In the morning he got ready for school.
Whenever Mom came in to check,
he had his boots on the wrong feet.

"Quickly, Quigley," said Quigley's Mom.
"And don't forget your hat and boots."

Quigley was small.
And Quigley was slow.
When he went to school he drew pictures.
Some days he lost his red crayon,
some days he lost his green crayon.

"Quickly, Quigley," said Quigley's teacher.
"Come join the class."

Quigley was small.
And Quigley was slow.

When the bell rang it was
time to play.
The little penguins ran outside;
he was always the last one.

"Quickly, Quigley," said Quigley's friends.
"Catch up."

Quigley was small.
And Quigley was slow.

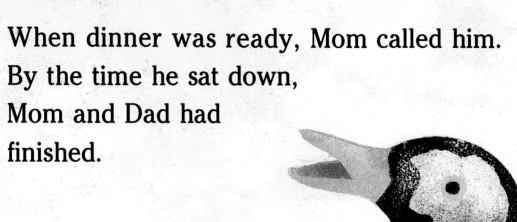

When dinner was ready, Mom called him.
By the time he sat down,
Mom and Dad had
finished.

"Quickly, Quigley," said Quigley's parents.
"Finish eating so you can play."

Quigley was small.
And Quigley was slow.
When it was bedtime,
there were toys all over the room,
and he was still playing.

"Quickly, Quigley," said Quigley's dad.
"Clean up, then I'll read to you."

Quigley was small.
And Quigley was slow.
One spring day his brother was born.
Things changed at home,
and he was busier than ever.

"Quickly, Quigley! Fetch the baby's shoes!"
"Quickly, Quigley! Get a blanket for your brother!"
"Quickly, Quigley!"

One day Quigley took his brother
to meet his friends.
"Quickly, Quigley!" they called.
Quigley was running to catch up
when he heard a small voice cry,
"Quigley...

slow down!"